PINOCCHIO

AND HIS PUPPET SHOW ADVENTURE

Random House ⌂ New York

Copyright © 1973 by Walt Disney Productions. All rights reserved under International and Pan-American Copyright Conventions. Published in the United States by Random House, Inc., New York, and simultaneously in Canada by Random House of Canada Limited, Toronto.

Library of Congress Cataloging in Publication Data

Disney (Walt) Productions.

Walt Disney's Pinocchio.

(Disney's wonderful world of reading. #10)

A simplified version of the classic tale of a talking wooden puppet whose nose grew long whenever he told a lie.

[1. Puppets and puppet-plays—Fiction.] 2. Fantasy. I. Lorenzini, Carlo, 1826-1890. Le avventure di Pinocchio. II. Title. III. Title: Pinocchio. PZ8.D632Wal15 [E] 73-395 ISBN 0-394-82626-4 ISBN 0-394-92626-9 (lib. bdg.)

Manufactured in the United States of America

2 3 4 5 6 7 8 9 0   Y Z

R

There was once a kind old man named
Geppetto. He lived in a little house
with his goldfish, Cleo, and his cat, Figaro.
Another friend, Jiminy Cricket, lived
in the house, too.

Geppetto could make wonderful things out of wood. One day he made a puppet that looked just like a boy. He called the puppet Pinocchio.

"How I wish Pinocchio was a *real* boy," he said. "It would be fun to have a son."

A good fairy heard Geppetto's wish.
That night she came to his house
when everyone was sleeping.
She touched Pinocchio with her wand.

Suddenly, the little wooden puppet
came to life.

And what did Pinocchio do first?

He tried to take Cleo out of the goldfish bowl!

"No, no, Pinocchio!" cried Jiminy Cricket. "Put that fish right back!"

The noise woke up Geppetto. He could not believe his eyes. There was his wooden puppet— singing and dancing!

The old man was so happy he hugged Pinocchio. "My son!" he said. "My own little wooden son!"

Geppetto wanted to cook breakfast for Pinocchio. But there was nothing to eat.

"Let me go out and buy some food, Father," said Pinocchio.

"My, my! What a good boy you are!" said
Geppetto. The old man gave Pinocchio some
money and a list of things to buy.

Jiminy Cricket was not so sure that
Pinocchio was a good boy. "I will just
follow him and see," he said to himself.

Pinocchio walked happily down the street.
He smiled at everybody. Everybody smiled at him.
It was fun to be out in the big world by himself.

A boy named Lampwick was also out by himself.
Lampwick was not a good boy. He told stories that
were not true. He even stole things.

When Lampwick saw Pinocchio, he said:

"Aha! I bet I can trick *that* wooden head."

"Hi, friend," said Lampwick.
"What do you have there?"
"Money," said Pinocchio.
"I am going
to buy food."

"Why not buy candy?"
said Lampwick.
"It tastes better."
"No, no! Pinocchio.
Don't listen," called
Jiminy Cricket.
Pinocchio paid no
attention. He followed
Lampwick to the
candy store.

"Where did you get so much money?"
asked the lady in the candy store.

"My father gave it to me," said Pinocchio.

"To buy candy?" asked the lady.

"Yes, to buy candy."

This was not true. Suddenly, Pinocchio's
nose started to grow longer.

He took his candy
out of the store as fast as
he could.

"Let *me* hold the bag," said Lampwick.
"It will be safer with me. I'm bigger."

Pinocchio held out the bag of candy.
To his surprise, Lampwick grabbed it and
ran away. That was the end of the candy!

"What happened?"
asked Jiminy.

"Where is all your
father's money?"

"I lost it,"
said Pinocchio.

Right away his nose grew still longer!

"You did *not* lose
the money," said Jiminy.
"You used it for candy.
Well, at least take
what is left and buy
a *little* food for Geppetto."

As he walked toward home, Pinocchio
held the bag of food in front of his face. He
did not want anyone to see his long nose.

A sly old fox and a thin, hungry cat
were hiding by a bridge.

"Look at that little wooden head," said
the hungry cat. "He has a sack of food."

"Hello, my fine lad," said the fox. "You look like just the sort of boy who might want to see a puppet show."

"A puppet show!" cried Pinocchio. "Oh, yes. I certainly would. How can I get in?"

"I have a ticket," said the fox. "If you
give us your food, I will give you my ticket.

"That *is* your sack of food, isn't it?"

"Oh, yes," said Pinocchio.

Another lie!
His nose grew longer yet.
But he didn't care.
He had his ticket.

A line of people were waiting to get into the puppet show. They got mad at Pinocchio when he bumped them with his long nose.

"Better not tell any more lies," said Jiminy Cricket. "You already have too much nose for a puppet your size."

"Step up! Step up!" called the man waiting at the ticket stand.

Pinocchio stepped up. He gave the man his ticket.

"This is no ticket," said the man.

"It's just a piece of paper. Go away, little boy, and take your long nose with you."

Poor Pinocchio!

He had no money, no food, no ticket.

He sat down on a box and began to cry.

Just then a man peeked out of the tent.

The man was Stromboli, the puppet master.

"My, my!" said Stromboli. "A puppet
without any strings. Can you do anything
but cry, little puppet?"

"I can dance and sing," said Pinocchio.
"Show me," said Stromboli.

Pinocchio
danced.

He sang.

He turned
cartwheels.

He even stood on his head.

Then Stromboli showed his puppets
to Pinocchio. He pulled their strings, and
the puppets kicked their feet.

"*You* don't need any strings," said Stromboli.
"Come with us. You will be the star of our show."

"Don't listen, Pinocchio. Go home to Geppetto,"
said Jiminy. But Pinocchio did not want to go home.
He wanted to be a star.

The show started, and Pinocchio began to dance.
"Look! No strings!" he called.
Everybody cheered.

But the other puppets had strings.
Pinocchio's long nose got caught
in those strings. He crashed to the floor.
Everybody started to laugh.

Suddenly Pinocchio was very unhappy.
He did not like to have people laugh at him.

"I am not such a great star
after all," he said.

"I want to go home
to Geppetto."

"Oh, no! You are not going home," said Stromboli. "You belong to me now. This bird cage will be your home, my little long-nosed friend."

"Help!" called Pinocchio from inside the cage. "Let me out!"

But the puppets could not help. They could not move unless someone pulled their strings.

Jiminy could not help either. He was too small. But he could *get* help.

Jiminy ran quickly to Geppetto's house.

"Geppetto!" he called. "You must come
save Pinocchio. Stromboli, the puppet master,
has put him in a cage."

"My poor little Pinocchio in a cage?"
said Geppetto.

The old man followed Jiminy
down the dark street.
He was carrying a lantern in one hand.

They found Pinocchio in his cage
in Stromboli's tent.

"Don't worry, my son," said Geppetto.
"I will help you." He opened the cage
and lifted Pinocchio out.

Suddenly, Stromboli came running.
"Thief!" he cried. "That is *my* puppet."

"Run, Pinocchio!" shouted Geppetto.

Pinocchio ran. Geppetto ran, too.

But the old man did not see the open trunk. He fell into it.

"Aha! Now I have you!" shouted Stromboli in a terrible voice.

"*I* will save you, Father!" called Pinocchio.
Quickly he went up a ladder to the place
where the puppets were hanging.

Pinocchio dropped the puppets—
strings and all—onto Stromboli. The puppet
master could not move. Geppetto was safe!

"My good, brave Pinocchio!" said Geppetto.
And he hugged his little son.

Fast as they could, Geppetto, Pinocchio and
Jiminy ran off toward home.

As soon as they were safe at home, Geppetto took a good look at Pinocchio.

"What has happened to your nose?" he cried.

"Tell him the truth now," said Jiminy.
This time Pinocchio did tell the truth.
He told Geppetto about everything —
just as it had happened.

While he talked, his nose got
shorter and shorter.

Finally it was just the way Geppetto
had made it.

Never again, Pinocchio decided, would he
tell another lie.